© Copyright 2021 Deana Meaux

ISBN: 978-0-578-97816-1

Author: Deana Meaux

Editor: Megan Southall

Illustrator: Cat Elliot

Photography: Cory Coreil

"I just want to be ME!"
Says
Achoo the Bee

Deana Meaux

There once was a bee
who was different, you see...
the day she was born
the other bees gave her scorn.

Achoo kept sneezing and blowing all the pollen away
that the worker bees collected from flowers in fields that day.

"I just can't stop sneezing," she moaned.
That's why the Queen named her Achoo from atop her throne.

"We worked so hard collecting the pollen!"
exclaimed a snarky bee named Olive.

"Please STOP sneezing you silly little bee
or you will blow the pollen to eternity!"

"Why can't you be like us?" cried Gus.

"I just want to be me," groaned Achoo the Bee.

The next flower Achoo flew to
she pinched her tiny nose to avoid a sneeze,
which felt like it was coming from the bottom of her little knees.

But oh, geez! That didn't work.
Her body went berserk!

Little wings flapping around
landing Achoo right onto the ground!

All the bees laughed watching Achoo take a tumble.
A shy bee named Bit heard a mumble,
"I just want to be me," Achoo the Bee grumbled.

The next day Achoo, eager to please
woke up before the other bees.

She exclaimed, "Today, I will NOT sneeze!"
and raced to the flower field with ease.

As she got closer to a flower,
she began to lose power.

"Uh-Oh!" Achoo could feel a sneeze come on,
and it was barely dawn!

Achoo heard a shy little voice:
"What are you doing out here at this hour?"

"Trying not to sneeze,"
Achoo said with unease.

"I wanted to practice not to sneeze around the flowers."
Bit thought, "But that's where she gets her amazing power."

All of a sudden, Achoo and Bit hear a buzzin'.

Gosh darn it - It's Clarence the Hornet!

Bit yelled, "He's heading for the hive!"
Achoo declared, "I have to warn the Queen or no one will get out alive!"

"But oh, my goodness! How can I do it?"
"There's nothing to it!" said Bit, showing a little grit.

"How can that be?" asked Achoo the Bee.

"I know a way you can save the day!" Bit said in a flit.
"You have a skill that everyone will envy;
use your sneeze to outrun the enemy!"

"Oh, thank you, Bit. That's it!"

Achoo found the nearest flower,
which gave her sneezing power.
Then with a big sniff,
she took off in a jiff.

But Clarence was super fast.
He took off in a flash!

Achoo was a flying pro but was a bit slow.
She realized, "I have to pick up my tempo."

She flew close to another pretty flower
that tickled her nose just right,
hoping this would allow her to sneeze with all of her might.

Achoo's giant sneeze pushed her past Clarence,
where she met the Queen in her room,
informing her of the coming doom.

The hive's heavy doors were shut in Clarence's face,
interrupting his extremely fast pace.

He hurt from his nose
all the way down to his toes.

The bees started to cheer as they patted Achoo on the back
for saving their home from Clarence's awful attack.

While the worker bees tied Clarence down,
Gus and Olive came around.

They told Achoo they felt sad
and hoped she wasn't mad.

Because they were sorry for not being nice
to the bee that saved their life.

Gus said, "Thank you for keeping us alive!
What will you do now? Guard the hive?"

Olive exclaimed, "Maybe you can be the Queen's right hand!
You will have a court, cooks, and a royal band!"

Achoo thought for a minute and imagined how life would be,
drinking daily tea
and living like royalty.

Then she shouted with glee,
"I don't want to be royalty,
I'm happy as can be,
just being me!"

Deana Meaux, Author

Notice anything similar between Achoo and Deana?

Deana came to appreciate her crazy, curly hair as something that didn't just make her different – it made her unique!

She loved reading colorful rhyming books to her three young children. One day she decided to write her own rhyming book about her experiences of standing out.

Now that her kids are grown, Deana decided to share her story with other young kids. Despite pressure on children to look a certain way in order to be accepted, she hopes every child will see themselves in Achoo and not be afraid to exclaim,

"I just want to be me!"

Follow Deana Meaux and Achoo the Bee

www.Facebook.com/AchooTheBee   www.Instagram.com/AchooTheBee   Info@DeanaMeaux.com

For more copies of Achoo the Bee please visit
www.AchooTheBee.com